JENNY

BY

Jean Poindexter Colby

WITH ILLUSTRATIONS BY

Marie C. Nichols

HASTINGS HOUSE, PUBLISHERS, NEW YORK

To my daughter Toni

who is largely responsible

for Jenny and this book.

COPYRIGHT, ©, 1957, BY JEAN POINDEXTER COLBY and MARIE C. NICHOLS

Library of Congress Catalog Card Number: 57-10732

Printed in the United States of America

It was a cold, damp day in late winter when the Clark family first saw their new home. It wasn't really new. In fact, it was an old Victorian house, painted a dark, gloomy gray and surrounded by tall pines that made it look even gloomier. The three children stood on the sidewalk and looked at it with their parents and tried to think of something nice to say about it.

"It's bigger than the apartment," said Alice, who was fourteen. "At least we will each have our own room. I won't have to sleep with Meg."

"I won't have to sleep with you, either," replied Meg with all her six-year-old independence.

But it was Pete, aged ten, who did see something good about it. "Look, Dad," he exclaimed, "at that cute old brass plate. It just says 27 CHESTNUT ST. It doesn't say 'No dogs and children allowed,' the way all the other places did. How about a dog, Dad?"

"Let's get moved in first," his father answered. "Anyway, a dog comes with the place. Look!" And he pointed to a figure under one of the pine trees. It was an old-fashioned iron dog on a small pedestal, a setter with one paw up and his tail out straight behind him.

He seemed to be eternally pointing something in the pine trees.

The children ran to the figure and Meg patted it. Pete looked it all over and suddenly shouted. "There are some words on the bottom of it, see?" He scraped away the pine needles and leaves at the base, disclosing the old-fashioned letters:

JENNY

A WISE AND LOVING MEMBER OF OUR FAMILY

1889 - 1910

They all stood silent for a moment. Then Pete said, "It's nice, but I meant a live dog."

Mr. Clark nodded. "I know. You can have one after we move in and get settled down a little. But it can't be an expensive dog. We've spent all our money on the house."

So one day, after what seemed a long, tiring time of moving in and unpacking, the Clark children and their mother went to the Angell Memorial Hospital in Boston to get a dog. That is where many lost and unwanted dogs are taken. If a person can prove he will be a good owner, he can have his pick of the day's dogs for seven dollars.

At first the Clarks were looking for a setter puppy like Jenny, but there wasn't any. There was a part-chow part-collie. And a grown boxer.

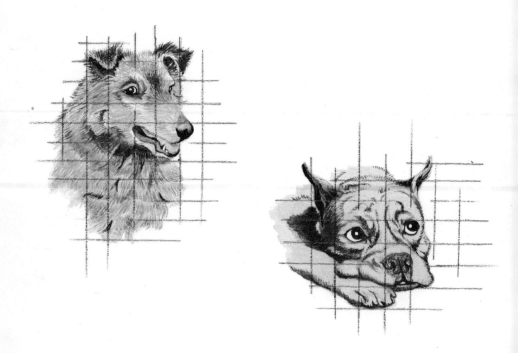

And a Great Dane with a broken leg. And a mother cat and five kittens. And *this* dog.

"I like this one," said Pete, stopping in front of one cage.

"So do I," agreed Meg, joining him.

"What kind is it?" asked Alice, a little scornfully.

"It says 'pointer' on the tag," answered Mother. "But she must be part something else, too."

"Her head is like a pointer's," Pete pointed out, "and so is her tail."

"And she has spots on her ankles like a pointer," Meg added.

"But the rest of her IS something else," Alice insisted, while Meg put two of her fingers in the cage.

The dog's eyes lit up; she quivered all over with gladness and lapped Meg's fingers with her long red tongue.

The little girl laughed with delight. "I don't care, it's a NICE something else. Let's get her."

"I don't know what Daddy will think of her," Mother answered slowly. "She isn't a setter and she isn't very handsome. But she has some bird dog in her and she is kind and friendly."

So Mother signed the papers and paid the seven dollars.

Outside, Pete asked, "What will we name her? Let's give her a good name."

Alice looked at the black-and-white dog and lifted her eyebrows in disdain. "She doesn't look very good out in the daylight. You can't name her Jenny, certainly. The other dog was a thoroughbred."

"That's not what it said," objected Meg stoutly. "It said 'wise and loving.' And that's what this Jenny might turn out to be."

"I think it's a good name for any kind of dog," Pete said slowly. "And it's a name that goes with the house."

"*She* goes with the house," Alice added crossly under her breath. "Shabby and wornout. Daddy isn't going to like her." But no one heard her. They were all trooping to the car with Jenny leading the way, lean and mangy but cavorting with joy, as if she knew already that she belonged to them.

They were all waiting with Jenny when Daddy drove home that afternoon. Meg was holding her. But just as Mr. Clark got out of the car, the dog smelled something, jumped away, and ran straight for some thick bushes in the back yard. Daddy watched. They all did.

"That's a funny-looking setter," grunted Daddy.

"It's a pointer," explained Pete.

"Some pointer!" Daddy's face was glum until suddenly Jenny wheeled around and *did* point! She must have smelled a bird in the bushes.

"For goodness' sakes!" cried Daddy. "It *is* a pointer. At least 10 per cent, anyway."

"You don't like her, do you, Daddy?" asked Alice.

Meg and Pete looked worried, but Daddy answered, "Sure, for a seven-dollar dog she's all right. Let's go in and wash up and have dinner. I'm hungry."

At first Jenny was not housebroken, so she had to be let out all the time. But she learned quickly. Meg taught her to bark to go out and Pete taught her to bark to come in. She thought that was fun, and for a while people were busy opening and shutting doors for her whenever she barked. Until Mother said that was *enough*.

Jenny seemed to understand, and only barked every fifteen minutes after that.

When she first came, she skidded on the rugs on the old waxed floors, but soon she learned which she could run on safely. And, while doing so, she found one in the front hall that she could really slide on and then the children would laugh. They would have her run the length of the hall, jump on that rug, and take off!

Mother had to put a stop to this sport, too, except every once in a while.

Soon Jenny took over as house guard. The house had long Victorian windows on the first floor that almost reached the ground. Jenny found them excellent observation posts. Every morning, when Daddy was having his breakfast, Jenny would sit near him, look out the window, and, as he said, "review the situation."

If she saw a squirrel, she would whine and lick her chops.

If she saw another dog, she would growl and bristle. The hair along her back would stand up in a funny little ridge.

If she saw Lottie, the cleaning woman, she would wag her tail and whine nice little whines.

But the worst was when the garbage man came. Then she almost went crazy. She would growl and bark and whine and tear to the back door. Then to the front door. And jump up and down. And no one could stop her.

"The garbage man must have kicked her!" Daddy shouted above the rumpus. "Let her out and see what happens."

"Never!" shouted Mother. "The insurance man would stop our insurance."

Soon, as the weeks went by, Jenny became more and more one of the family. Even Alice got to like her although she wouldn't admit it to her brother and sister.

One day Alice said, "You must learn some tricks, Jenny."

Jenny gave her a suspicious look. Alice was strict, sometimes stricter than Mother.

They went into the kitchen and Alice got a few pieces of dog biscuit to give her as a reward. "Beg, Jenny, beg." And she pushed her up on her tail. But the dog's rump seemed too round and she fell over. Alice held out the biscuit. "Beg, Jenny, beg. Beg, Jenny, beg." Again she pushed her up and again she fell over. "Beg, Jenny, beg. Beg, Jenny, beg." The words went on and on. The result was the same.

"Mother," Peter called down from upstairs, "I can't study with that beg business going on."

"Even the garbage-man racket is better than that!" shouted Daddy.

"I'll put on the vacuum cleaner and drown them out," said Mother.

So the house got very clean the next few days, until suddenly Jenny rolled her eyes and gave up resisting the training. She begged beautifully.

In the same way Alice taught her to roll over. But sometimes Jenny got mixed up and wouldn't go all the way over. She just rolled around on the floor on her back, playing. Then Alice was stern. She kept calling, "Roll over, Jenny. Roll over, Jenny," until Daddy said, "Do you think Alice would stop saying that if *I* rolled over?"

Soon Jenny learned to roll over nicely, too.

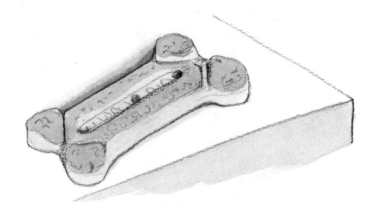

Then Jenny learned to be "dead dog." This was funny because Jenny would lie out flat, very still, until Alice reached up on the table for the dog biscuit, then Jenny would open one eye and shut it quickly before Alice saw her. Everybody came out to the kitchen to see that part.

And Daddy added another funny thing to the dead-dog trick. He had gone to Harvard College, and when some of his friends visited him, he would ask Jenny, "Would you rather die or go to Yale?" and Jenny would stretch out on the floor as dead looking as can be! The men would laugh and laugh.

Pete got interested in the trick business, too. He decided to teach Jenny to bring in the morning paper. The dog got the idea right away, but first she snatched the paper and ran all over the yard with it. Then she would bring it inside and run all over the house with it.

Finally she learned to put it on Mr. Clark's footstool and afterward she would bark and bark in delight as if saying, "Look what I can do!"

Gradually the Clark family and Jenny settled into their new house. They found the right places for things. They painted the kitchen and bathroom and got all their pictures hung and a special bed for Jenny made in the laundry.

One day in the spring Mother told the family, "It's almost Easter. We've all worked hard and the house looks nice. We ought to ask some of the neighbors in. Let's start with the minister. He has called on us and we should have him to dinner."

"Fine," said Daddy. "He seems a nice fellow. Let's have something good to eat—like roast beef."

The mention of the dinner gave Meg an idea. Everyone had taught Jenny a trick except her and, of course, they would show all the tricks off the night of the minister's visit and Meg wanted to have a part in the fun. She tried to think what the minister would like to see. At her old home their former clergyman had come often for dinner but he had acted just like anyone else except he said grace instead of Daddy at the table.

So Meg decided she would teach Jenny to pray just like the rest of the family when grace was said. That would be proper for a minister's visit.

She worked on the idea down in the laundry, trying to get Jenny to come up to her and put her head in her lap while she said grace. At first Jenny, who had grown a lot in the last three months, jumped right up in her lap

and knocked her over. The second time she put her head in Meg's lap but rolled her eyes while grace was said. Jenny was a good eye-roller.

But at last she did her job just right and Meg gave her a nice big gobbet of hamburger out of the icebox in reward.

When the day came for the minister's visit, Meg gave Jenny a bath and put a white ribbon on her collar. The dog seemed to know it was a special day and capered around, whining softly with pleasure.

When the minister arrived, Jenny was brought out and introduced and put through her tricks. She begged, and rolled over, and played dead dog, and brought in the evening paper.

Then when they went in to dinner Meg said, "I have a new trick that I taught Jenny. Here, Jenny. Come, Jenny."

The dog came obediently and sat looking up at her. "Pray, Jenny."

Whereupon the dog put her head in Meg's lap and closed her eyes. Meg said grace correctly and when she got to the "Amen" Jenny opened her eyes and looked around.

There was complete silence. Daddy was red in the face, Mother looked very queer, and Alice and Pete stood with their mouths open.

Suddenly there was a hearty laugh. It was the minister. "That's wonderful! She does it very reverently and well."

Daddy let out his breath in a little explosion. "Do forgive the child. She meant no wrong."

"Of course she didn't," said the minister. "That dog is almost as smart as a human being and there is no reason why the two shouldn't pray together. May their prayers be answered. And now let us *all* pray.

"Oh heavenly Father, who hast blessed us with the joy and care of children, give us light and strength to lead them in the paths of righteousness. Help us to enjoy the world of nature and dumb animals with them that they may love whatsoever things are true and pure and lovely, following the example of their Saviour, Jesus Christ. Amen."

Then they all began dinner.

"Boy, was that ever a surprise!" burst out Pete, over-come with admiration and wonder for his younger sister and their dog.

Even Alice looked impressed. "Jenny is wise and loving just like the first Jenny, isn't she, Daddy?"

"And a member of our family even though she isn't what Alice said—a thoroughbred. Isn't she, Daddy?" asked Mcg.

"She is Jenny Clark from now on," answered Daddy.

"Amen to that," added the minister.

At which Jenny gave a great bark and took off down the hall, heading for her pet sliding rug.

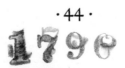